llama llama misses mama

to Maw, Maw
B.

the best
grandmom
in the
world!!!!!!

I Love
You!!!

llama llama misses mama

Anna Dewdney

SCHOLASTIC INC.
New York Toronto London Auckland
Sydney Mexico City New Delhi Hong Kong

Llama Llama, warm in bed.
Wakey, wakey, sleepyhead!

Llama school begins **today**!
Time to learn and time to play!

Make the bed and
find some clothes.

Brush the teeth
and blow the nose.

Eat some breakfast.
Clean the plate.

Whoops!
Oh my—
we're running late!

Drive to school
and park the car.

Tell the teacher
who you are.

Meet new faces.
Hear new names.
See new places.
Watch new games.

Hang the coat
and say good-bye.

Llama Llama
feeling shy. . . .

Mama Llama goes away.
Llama Llama has to stay.

Strange new teacher.
Strange new toys.
Lots of kids
and lots of noise!

What would Llama like to do?
Llama Llama feels so new. . . .

Build a castle out of blocks?
Make a rocket from a box?
Llama Llama shakes his head.
Llama walks away instead.

Here's a little chugga-choo
with a captain and a crew.
Would the llama like a ride?
Llama Llama tries to hide.

Reading stories on the rug.
Kids are cuddled, sitting snug.

Would the llama like to look?

Llama Llama
hates that book.

Time for lunch! Now find a seat.

Llama doesn't want to eat.
Llama makes a little moan.
Llama Llama feels **alone.**

Llama misses Mama so. . . .

Why did Mama Llama **go?**

It's too much
for little Llama . . .

Llama Llama **MISSES MAMA!**

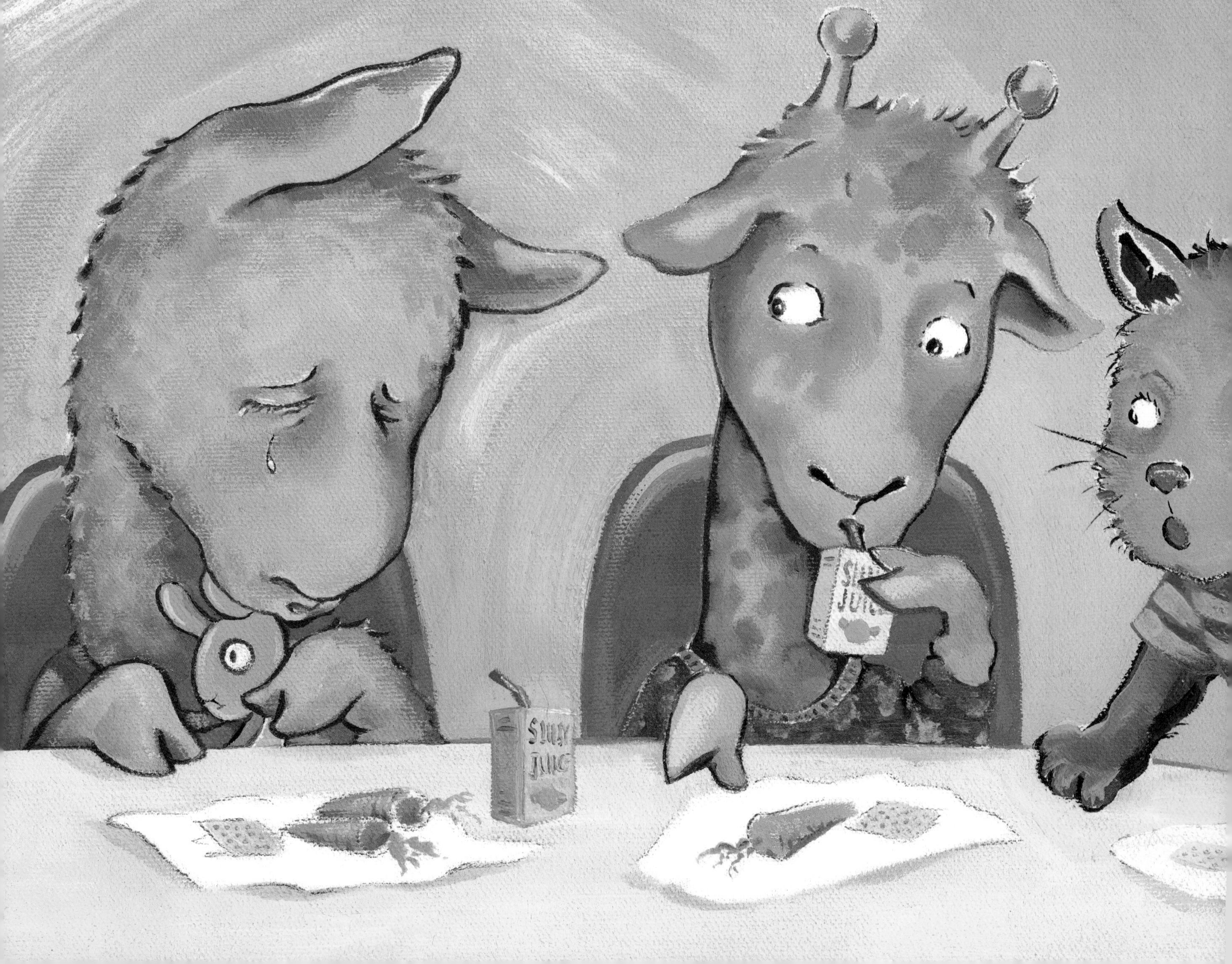

Don't be sad, new little llama!
It's OK to miss your mama.
But don't forget—
when day is through,

she will come **right back** to you.

Llama Llama, please don't fuss.
Have some fun and play with **us!**

Put on coats and run outside.
See the playhouse! Try the slide.

Tag and jump rope. Hide and seek.
Close your eyes and do not peek!

Now it's time to
draw and write.
Great big crayons.
Colors bright.

Take some paper
from the stack . . .

MAMA
LLAMA!

Teacher gets a good-bye hug.

Wave to friends on reading rug.

Climb the playhouse with the slide.
See if Mama fits inside.

Lots to show and lots to say!
Back again another day. . . .

Llama finds out something new—

He loves Mama . . .

and **SCHOOL**, too!

For Berol, my first to go off to school

ISBN 978-0-545-28604-6

12 11 10 9 8 7 6 5 4 3 2   10 11 12 13 14 15/0

Printed in the U.S.A.   08

This edition first printing, September 2010

Set in ITC Quorum